T is for Thor

A Norse Mythology Alphabet

D1174820

Written by Virginia Loh-Hagan ∗ Illustrated by Torstein Nordstrand

Glossary

The Norse World

Alfheim (/alf-haym/): one of the nine realms, where the elves lived

Asgard (/ass-guard/): one of the nine realms, where the Aesir gods and goddesses lived

Gimle (/gim-lee/): one of the nine realms, known as the high heavens

Helheim (/hell-haym/): part of Niflheim, which was ruled by Hel and housed all the souls of those who did not die in battle

Jotunheim (/your-turn-haym/): one of the nine realms, where Norse giants lived

Midgard (/mid-guard/): one of the nine realms, where humans lived

Muspell (moo-spell/): one of the nine realms, where the fire giants lived

Niflheim (/niff-el-haym/): one of the nine realms, located at the lowest level and with ice and snow

Svartalfheim (/svart-ald-haym/): one of the nine realms, where the dwarfs lived

Vanaheim (/varna-haym/): one of the nine realms, where the Vanir gods and goddesses lived

Yggdrasil (/eeg-drass-ill/): the world tree, which housed all nine realms of Norse mythology and which had three enormous roots

Norse Halls

Bilskirnir (/bill-skin-ya/): Thor's hall, which means "lightning crack"

Fensalir (/fan-sah-lere/): Frigg's hall, which was in a marsh

Sessrumnir (/sass-roo-mere/): Freya's hall, which housed warrior souls that didn't go to Valhalla

Norse Halls (*continued*)

Valaskjalf (/va-lah-ah-skelf/): one of Odin's halls, which housed his and Frigg's thrones

Valhalla (/val-hal-lah/): one of Odin's halls, which housed the souls of brave warriors

Norse Beings

Aesir (/eye-sear/): gods and goddesses who ruled over humans, wars, storms, and skies and who lived in Asgard

Austri (/irst-tree/): one of four dwarfs sent by Odin to the four corners of Ymir's skull

Dwarfs (/dworfs/): creatures who were skilled craftsmen and lived in the mountains or underground in Svartalfheim

Einherjar (/in-here-ee-yar/): souls of brave dead warriors who lived and trained at Valhalla

Jotnar (/yot-nar/): giants who lived in Jotunheim

Nordri (/nor-dree/): one of four dwarfs sent by Odin to the four corners of Ymir's skull

Norns (/norns/): Nordic seers who practiced seidr and ruled over the fates of gods and men

Sudri (/soo-dri/): one of four dwarfs sent by Odin to the four corners of Ymir's skull

Vanir (/var-near/): gods and goddesses of nature and fertility who lived in Vanaheim

Vestri (/vest-tree/): one of four dwarfs sent by Odin to the four corners of Ymir's skull

Norse Gods

Balder (/bal-durr/): god of light and sunshine

Bor (/bore/): Buri's son and Odin's father

Norse Gods (*continued*)

Bragi (/brag-ee/): god of poetry and Idunn's husband

Buri (/boo-ree/): the first Aesir god

Freya (/fray-ah/): Vanir goddess of love, beauty, war, and death, who lived with the Aesir as a hostage

Frey (/fray/): Vanir god of good fortune, sunshine, seasons, and peace, who lived with the Aesir as a hostage

Frigg (/frig/): Odin's wife and queen of the Aesir

Heimdall (/haym-dahl/): god who served as the watchman of the gods by guarding Bifrost

Hlin (/he-lene/): one of Frigg's twelve maidens, whose job was to protect those whom Frigg selected

Hod (/hodd/): god of darkness who was the blind twin brother of Balder

Idunn (/eh-dunn/): goddess of youth, who guarded the golden apples of immortality

Kvasir (/kvahss-ere/): wisest of all Aesir and Vanir gods, who brought poetry to mankind

Mimir (/mee-mere/): wise Aesir god

Odin (/oh-din/): Bor's son and the ruler of the Aesir gods, who created the universe

Sif (/siff/): Thor's wife

Thor (/thore/): god of thunder and Odin's son

Norse Giants

Aegir (/eh-geer/): sea giant who ruled over the northern seas

Gerd (/gurd/): giantess who shone as bright as the sun

Norse Giants (continued)

Jord (/yord/): giantess who was the mother of Thor

Loki (/low-key/): trickster god who lived among the Aesir until he was exiled

Ran (/rawn/): giantess who ruled the seas

Surtr (/sert-ah/): fire giant who destroyed the Norse world during Ragnarok

Thiazi (/thee-ah-see/): storm giant

Ymir (/ee-mere/): frost giant who was the first being in the Norse world

Norse Creatures/Monsters

Audhumla (/oud-hoom-la/): cow that produced rivers of milk and brought Buri into being

Fenrir (/fen-rear/): giant wolf that kept growing and was one of Loki's monster children

Hel (/hell/): ruler of Helheim and one of Loki's monster children

Jormungundr (/your-moon-gand-ah/): giant world serpent that was one of Loki's monster children

Valkyries (/val-ker-ees/): young battle maidens whose name means "choosers of the slain"

Norse Humans

Ask (/ask/): one of the first two humans, who was made from an ash tree

Embla (/em-bler/): one of the first two humans, who was made from an elm tree

Lif (/leaf/): human woman who survived Ragnarok and whose name means "life"

Lifthrasir (/leaf-thrass-ear/): human man who survived Ragnarok and whose name means "life's zest"

Norse Landmarks

Bifrost (/bye-frost/): shimmering rainbow bridge connecting Asgard and Midgard

Elivagar (/ay-ea-vay-gar/): collective name of eleven poisonous rivers in Niflheim

Folkvangr (/folk-van-ger/): special meadow that belonged to Freya

Ginnungagap (/gin-noon-gah-gahp/): large void in which the world was created

Gjallarbru (/gee-yal-ler-brew/): covered bridge made of glittering gold that spanned over the Gjoll river

Gjoll (/gee-yoll/): one of Elivagar's poisonous rivers

Hvergelmir (/he-ver-gell-mere/): a well located in Niflheim; its name means "bubbling cauldron"

Mimisbrunnr (/mee-meres-broon-ah/): Mimir's Well of Knowledge, which was close to Jotunheim

Vigrid (/vee-grid/): battlefield where Ragnarok took place

Well of Urd (/oord/): a well that was taken care of by the Norns; known as the "Well of Fate"

Norse Weapons

Gjallerhorn (/gee-yal-ler-horn/): famous yelling horn used to signal the start of Ragnarok

Gungnir (/goong-near/): Odin's magical spear that never missed and always killed its targets

Mjollnir (/mee-oll-near/): Thor's hammer; its name means "the crusher"

Tyrfing (/tier-fing/): magical sword that had perfect aim and could fight by itself

Other Important Concepts

Fimbulwinter (/fimm-bull-vin-ter/): long period of harsh darkness and winter that signaled the start of Ragnarok

Prose Edda and ***Poetic Edda*** (/ed-uh/): ancient texts that provide much of what we know about Norse mythology, history, and religion

Ragnarok (/rag-na-rock/): great apocalyptic war that was prophesized to destroy the Norse world

Seidr (/say-der/): Norse sorcery or old folk magic

Skuld (/schooled/): future, also one of the three Norns

Urd (/oord/): past, also one of the three Norns

Verdandi (/vair-done-dee/): present, also one of the three Norns

Norse refers to areas in northern Europe, including Norway, Sweden, and Iceland. Ancient Norse people believed that powerful gods and goddesses ruled over all. The most powerful lived in Asgard, one of the realms (worlds) in Norse mythology. It was believed that the universe was separated into nine realms, which were held together by Yggdrasil, the world tree (the tree of life). Each realm had its own type of beings and its own purposes. With the exception of Asgard, the beings moved among the realms by climbing up or down Yggdrasil.

Norse mythology had three main types of beings: Jotnar, Vanir, and Aesir. The Jotnar were giants who lived in a realm called Jotunheim. The Vanir were nature gods associated with fertility and had powers to see the future. They lived in a realm called Vanaheim. The Aesir gods ruled over humans, wars, storms, and skies. They lived in Asgard, and many myths took place there.

The Aesir fought the Vanir for power over the nine realms. After a long war, a truce was declared, and the Aesir and Vanir traded hostages as part of a peace treaty. The realms coexisted until Ragnarok, a great war that destroyed the Norse world.

A a

A is for Asgard

Filled with fields of green
and castles of gold,
Asgard was home
to the strong and the bold.

B is for Bifrost

Spanning the worlds
of gods, giants, and men,
Bifrost, the rainbow bridge,
was Heimdall's to defend.

Asgard served as a fortress into which only
gods were allowed to enter by crossing
Bifrost, a shimmering rainbow bridge. Bifro
was surrounded by flames, which defendec
from intruders, melting away frost giants a
turning others into ashes.

The Aesir used Bifrost to travel around the
nine realms. Bifrost also served as a bridg
connecting Midgard and Asgard. Midgard w
the world of humans and was modeled afte
Asgard. Bifrost was the only connection
between the humans and gods.

In Asgard, it was the job of Heimdall, the
watchman of the gods, to guard Bifrost.
Bifrost was located at Heimdall's palace or
hall, high in the sky. Heimdall sat on top of
Bifrost and watched over all nine realms. He
could move between the realms, see the
future, and change forms, along with having
other powers. He didn't need to sleep, which
allowed him to be on guard all the time.

In many Norse myths, weapons had their
own names and stories. For example,
Heimdall had a magical "yelling horn" calle
Gjallerhorn, which could be heard in all nin
realms to summon the gods to battle.

C is for Creation Myth

From fire and ice
and one little spark,
a frost giant was born,
bringing life from the dark.

In the beginning, there was only a chaotic dark tornado of fire and ice. The fire and ice met in a large void called Ginnungagap. Sparks flew and some became the sun, moon, and stars. One spark melted ice and turned into Ymir, a frost giant who was the first being. Audhumla, a cow that produced rivers of milk, soon emerged. Ymir's sweat turned into more frost giants, who became the first rulers.

Audhumla licked salty ice for three days, bringing into being Buri, the first Aesir god. Buri had a son named Bor, who married a frost giant's daughter and had three Aesir sons, one of whom was Odin.

Odin and his brothers killed Ymir, claiming lands for Aesir gods and thus creating the nine realms. Ymir's death made all life possible. (In some stories, Yggdrasil emerged from Ymir's body.) Odin used Ymir's body parts to create everything in the universe. Ymir's blood became the seas and his flesh became soil. His bones became mountains and his hair became forests. Odin created more Aesir gods and created humans to worship the gods. By breathing life into trees, he created the first humans, Ask, meaning "ash tree," and Embla, meaning "elm tree."

Cc

As part of the creation myth, Odin turned Ymir's skull into the sky and his brains into clouds. Then, from the maggots that fed on Ymir's dead body, Odin created dwarfs. He sent four dwarfs to the four corners of Ymir's skull in order to ensure the sky arched over the earth. These dwarfs' names were Austri, which means "east"; Vestri, which means "west"; Nordri, which means "north"; and Sudri, which means "south." Other dwarfs were sent to live in the mountains or underground in a realm called Svartalfheim.

Dwarfs were talented craftsmen with secret knowledge and magical powers. They made weapons and charms for the gods and goddesses. One famed weapon was a magical sword named Tyrfing. This sword could fight by itself and its aim was always accurate. They also created a magical gold ring. From it, eight gold rings sprang out every ninth day, making its owner very rich.

Dwarfs were fierce and brave warriors, so they were often hired to defend treasures and fight in battles. They were also known to be vindictive and would hex and curse anyone who wronged them.

Dd

D is for Dwarfs

As craftsmen, dwarfs' skills
were second to none.
Using one of their swords,
many battles were won.

Ee

Elivagar is the collective name of eleven poisonous rivers. These rivers came from Hvergelmir, a well in Niflheim, which was the realm of ice and snow at the lowest level of the Norse universe. These rivers flowed from north to south. They had fearsome names that described their characteristics, such as boiling, freezing, and lightning. One of the rivers was named Gjoll, which means "a resounding scream." Gjoll separated the living from the dead, and flowed near the gates of hell. The dead had to cross the Gjallarbru (a covered bridge made of glittering gold) over Gjoll in order to reach the underworld.

In some stories, Elivagar is part of the creation myth. These rivers are thought to have existed since the beginning of the Norse universe. They are believed to be part of the tornado of fire and ice that clashed in Ginnungagap. Ymir, the first frost giant, was partly formed from the Elivagar waters.

Elivagar was known for being poisonous due to the many venomous snakes that swam in its freezing waters. The snakes' venom hardened in the water and floated in the rivers like bits of ice. In fact, Elivagar means "ice waves."

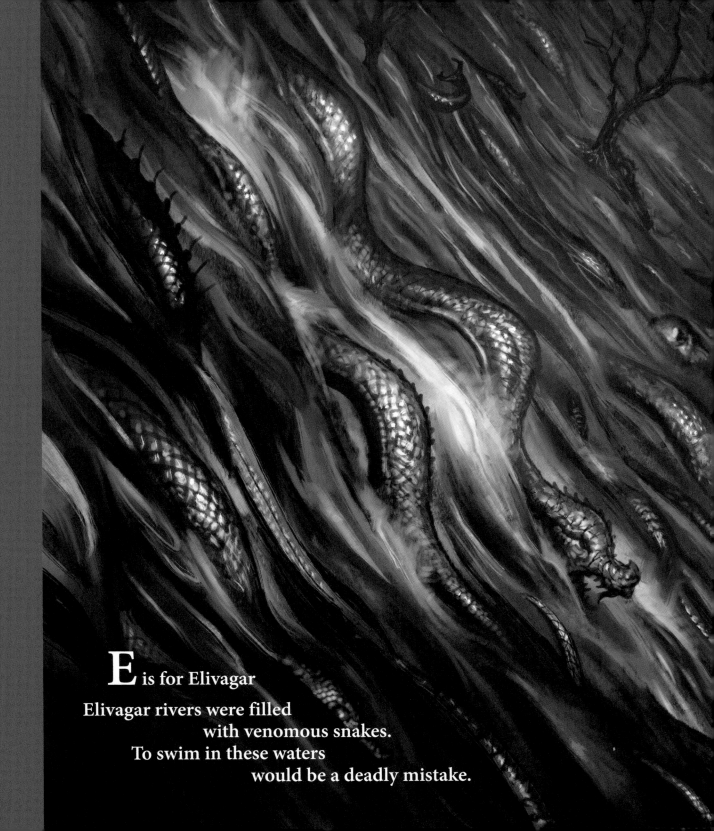

E is for Elivagar

Elivagar rivers were filled
with venomous snakes.
To swim in these waters
would be a deadly mistake.

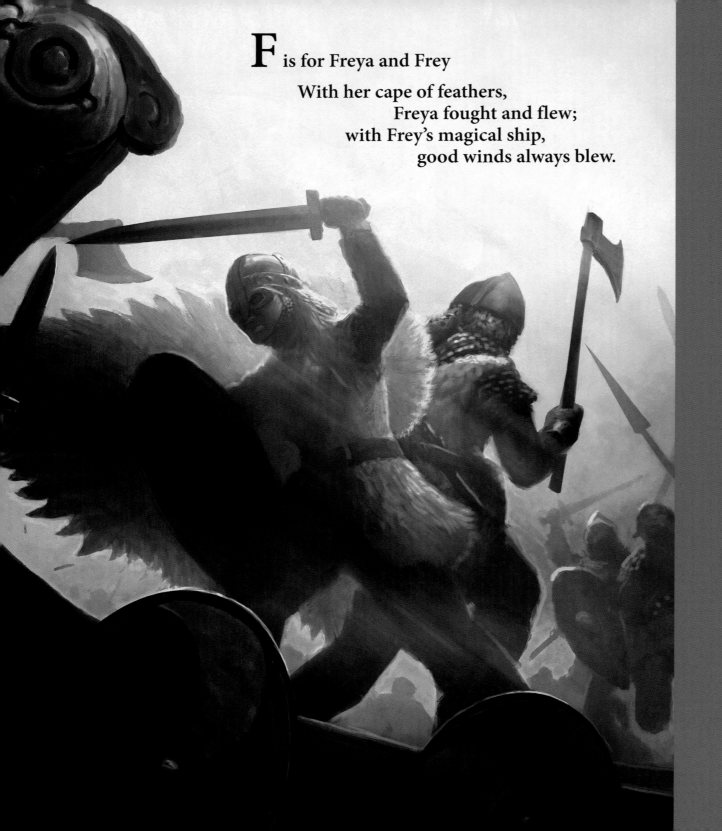

F is for Freya and Frey

With her cape of feathers,
   Freya fought and flew;
with Frey's magical ship,
   good winds always blew.

Freya and Frey were twins. Freya was the goddess of love, beauty, war, and death. Frey was the god of good fortune, sunshine, seasons, and peace. They were originally Vanir gods. But after the Aesir—Vanir war, they were among the hostages traded to the Aesir.

Freya practiced seidr, which was Norse sorcery or old folk magic. She taught seidr to some of the Aesir, upsetting the main gods, who saw this as an insult to their new reign. According to some sources, as punishment the Aesir tried three times to kill Freya by burning her. But she wouldn't die and kept rising from the ashes.

Freya and Frey had magical chariots. Freya's was pulled by big cats; Frey's was pulled by golden boars. When he rode in his chariot, Frey brought peace and prosperity to the land. Freya and Frey also had powerful weapons. Freya had a cloak made of falcon feathers that enabled her to fly. In some stories, the cloak turned its wearer into a falcon. Frey had a ship and whenever it flew, there was good weather. It took its passengers wherever they wanted to go and could be folded up and carried in a pocket.

G is for Giants and Gods

Norse gods and giants
were formidable foes;
until the gods conquered the giants,
so the story goes.

In many myths, Jotnar (giants) and gods were enemies. They fought and tricked each other, maintaining the balance between good and evil. The giants hated the gods, who had defeated Ymir.

In some myths, gods and giants helped each other. Some even got married. For example, in one story Frey fell in love with a giantess named Gerd. But Gerd didn't love Frey in return. Frey had a magical sword that could fight by itself and was always victorious. Desperate, he traded his sword for magic, which he used to make Gerd love him.

Gods could marry giantesses, but giants weren't allowed to marry goddesses. In one myth, Aesir gods hired a giant to build a wall around Asgard. In return, the giant wanted to marry Freya. Loki, the trickster god, came up with a scheme, promising the giant that he could marry Freya if he built the wall in one season. The giant agreed, but only if his horse could help. As it turned out, his horse was magical. To stop the giant from winning, Loki turned into a mare and lured the other horse away. Without his horse, the giant couldn't finish the wall.

Gg

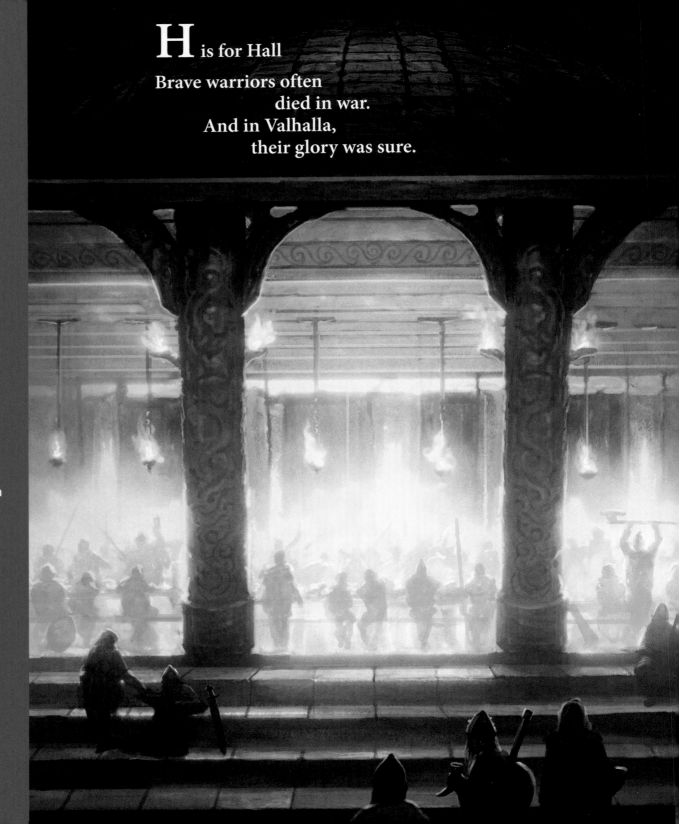

H h

Brave warriors often
died in war.
And in Valhalla,
their glory was sure.

Each of the main Aesir gods and goddesses had their own grand hall in Asgard. Valhalla (the "hall of the slain") was its most famous. It was one of Odin's palaces and was enormous. Dying in battle was the highest honor and the best warriors were sent to Valhalla. These dead warriors' souls were called Einherjar.

All gods knew of the Ragnarok prophecy, an apocalyptic war predicted to end the gods' reign and lead to the rebirth of a new world. The gods were prepared to die in Ragnarok to prevent evil from coming into the new world. As part of the gods' preparation, Einherjar were recruited to fight in Odin's army. During the day they trained and at night their wounds healed. There was plenty of food, as the warriors were served meat from a magical boar that was killed and came back to life every night.

Another famous hall in Asgard was Sessrumnir, which means "room of seats." It was Freya's palace in a special meadow called Folkvangr, which means "field of warriors." Freya claimed the souls of warriors who didn't go to Valhalla. She recruited them for her army to fight in Ragnarok.

Idunn was the Norse goddess of youth. She was married to Bragi, the god of poetry. Idunn had a magical orchard in Asgard and was the keeper of the golden apples of immortality. The Norse gods and goddesses were not immortal. They needed to eat Idunn's apples to stay young, healthy, and powerful. Idunn kept these apples in an ash-wood chest.

Everyone wanted her apples, especially a storm giant named Thiazi, who forced Loki to help him kidnap Idunn. Loki lured Idunn into the woods, where Thiazi kidnapped her, taking her to Jotunheim. Without Idunn's apples, the gods and goddesses started to age. They figured Loki was involved, and threatened to kill him unless he rescued Idunn.

Loki borrowed Freya's cloak and turned into a falcon. He found Idunn and changed her into a nut, flying off with her in his claws. When Thiazi found out, he became enraged and changed into an eagle, chasing after Loki. To help Loki, the gods built a big fire. Loki led Thiazi into the flames. To ensure his death, Thor, the god of thunder, killed Thiazi with his hammer. The gods would do anything to keep Idunn safe.

I i

I is for Idunn

Humans aged and aged,
growing old and gray.
But Idunn's apples
stopped the gods' decay.

J is for the Journey of Life and Death

After starting one's journey
to the realm of the dead,
Norse afterlife was based
on the life one had led.

Jj

The journey from life to death was an important part of ancient Norse beliefs. Besides Valhalla and Sessrumnir, which were located in Asgard, there were other places where dead souls could go. Those who didn't die in battle but from things such as sickness, old age, or accidents were sent to the underworld, Helheim, a part of Niflheim, which was the lowest level of the universe. Those who didn't worship the gods were also sent to Helheim. Helheim was immense, housing most of the dead souls from all nine realms.

The souls sent to Helheim had to cross the Gjallarbru, the bridge between the living and the dead. The souls in Helheim could never leave as they were trapped by the river Gjoll.

Those who died at sea went to live with the giantess Ran in her hall at the ocean floor. Ran ruled the seas and was known for drowning sailors and stealing ships full of treasure. Because sea life was difficult and dangerous, explorers and sailors were as honorable as warriors. Many sailors wanted to die at sea and would drown with their ships. Ships symbolized safe passage into the afterlife.

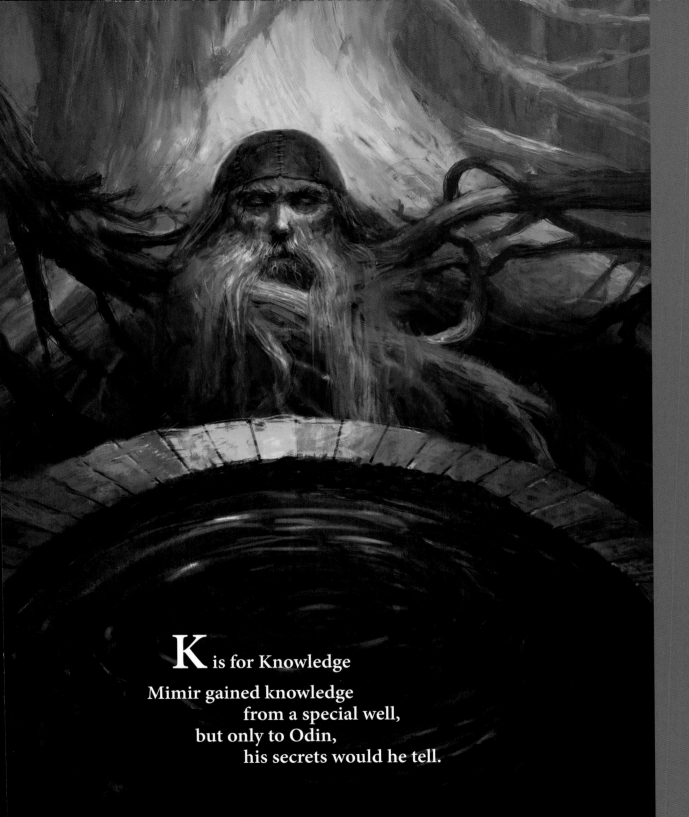

Mimir was a wise Aesir god. He was the guardian of the world's memory and of Mimisbrunnr, also called Mimir's Well of Knowledge. The well was located beneath Yggdrasil, the world tree, and close to Jotunheim. Only Mimir drank from this well, gaining great wisdom.

After the Aesir—Vanir war, the Aesir sent Mimir as a hostage to the Vanir as part of the peace treaty. The Vanir thought the exchange was unfair, as they had given the Aesir more valuable hostages (Freya and Frey). The Vanir beheaded Mimir and sent the head to Odin. Mimir's head could still talk and think so Odin kept it alive, preserving it with herbs and using charms and magic to give it power. Mimir's head gave Odin secret knowledge and sage advice.

The Aesir—Vanir peace treaty also required both parties to spit in a large pot, binding both forces together. From this spit emerged Kvasir, the wisest of all the Aesir and Vanir gods. Kvasir became a traveler, sharing his wisdom, until he was killed by dwarfs. They mixed his blood with honey, making a potion that enabled its drinkers to recite beautiful poetry. It is believed that Kvasir introduced poetry to mankind.

K is for Knowledge

Mimir gained knowledge
from a special well,
but only to Odin,
his secrets would he tell.

K k

Loki was the god of fire and magic, as well as chaos and trouble. He's best known for being a trickster god. He caused mayhem and mischief by lying and cheating. One of his greatest powers was his ability to transform into any living being.

In some stories, Loki was thought to be Odin's adopted son or his brother. But in most traditional Norse myths, Loki was the son of frost giants. However, he didn't live in Jotunheim. He lived among the gods in Asgard, where he liked to stir things up.

He loved to make trouble and then fix things so he could look like a hero. For example, once when he was bored, Loki played a trick on Thor's wife, Sif. She had beautiful golden hair. Loki snuck into Sif's room as she slept and he cut off her hair. When Thor found out, he sought revenge, but Loki convinced Thor to give him a chance to redeem himself. Loki made a deal with the dwarfs and had them create a majestic golden headpiece for Sif. This headpiece was even more beautiful than her real hair, which pleased both Thor and Sif.

L 16

L is for Loki

Sly Loki played
trick after trick.
To beat him, gods had to be
clever and quick.

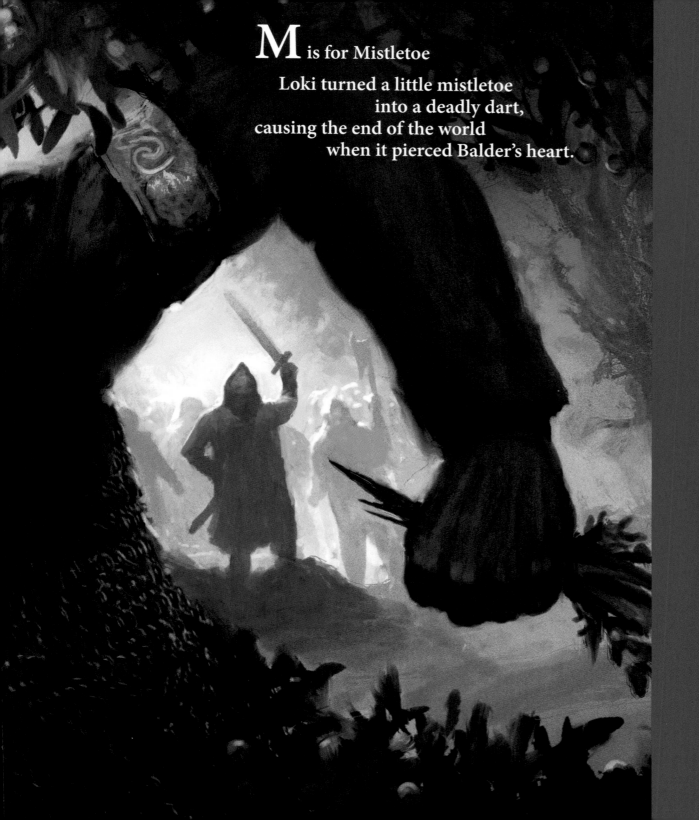

M is for Mistletoe

Loki turned a little mistletoe
into a deadly dart,
causing the end of the world
when it pierced Balder's heart.

Balder was the beloved god of light and sunshine and son of Odin and Frigg. He had premonitions of dying, which worried his mother. As queen, Frigg commanded all living things not to hurt Balder. But she overlooked the mistletoe plant, thinking it was too small to do harm. To test Balder's protection, Frigg held a party where the attending gods threw sharp objects at him. Because of Frigg's command, things bounced off Balder, leaving him unharmed. Loki, upset at not being invited, made a poisonous mistletoe dart and gave it to Hod. Hod was the god of darkness and Balder's blind twin brother. Loki guided Hod's hand as he threw the dart. It killed Balder, sending him to Helheim.

When Balder died, his light was extinguished, bringing on a great winter. This marked the beginning of Ragnarok. Hod was later killed by another Norse god seeking to avenge Balder's death. Hel, the ruler of Helheim, said Balder could return if all living things grieved him. All did except for Loki. The angry gods exiled Loki to a cave in the underworld, where he was tortured until Ragnarok.

M
m

N n

N is for Norns

Three magical Norns
spin and weave,
controlling fates that
none can leave.

The Norns were the three Nordic seers who practiced seidr, old Norse sorcery. They were powerful giantesses who ruled over the fates of gods and men. Their names were Urd, which means "past"; Verdandi, which means "present"; and Skuld, which means "future."

The Norns lived in a great hall by the Well of Urd, also known as the Well of Fate (not to be confused with Mimir's Well of Knowledge). The Norns' well was under Yggdrasil, and the seers served as the tree's caretakers. They drew magical water from the well and mixed it with the sand that surrounded it. They poured this mixture over Yggdrasil to ensure the tree's roots did not rot. They began each morning by placing a rooster on top of the tree. This was the wake-up call for all of Asgard.

The Norns were fortune-tellers and expert weavers, spinning the threads of life. They weaved people's fates into a web. Each person's life was a string in their loom and the length of the string was the length of a person's life. They attended births and determined whether the babies would have good or difficult lives.

As part of the creation myth, Odin was known as the all-father. His most famous children included Thor, Heimdall, Balder, and Hod.

Odin was the most powerful god and had an all-seeing eye. To be a good ruler, Odin knew he had to be wise. So he asked to drink from Mimir's Well of Knowledge, agreeing to sacrifice one of his eyes. Odin placed his eye in Mimir's well. His remaining eye became extremely powerful and had the ability to see everything, including the future and the past. His keen vision allowed him to foresee Ragnarok and thus, warn the gods. He also foresaw his death at Ragnarok.

Odin could travel into the minds of all beings and see their memories and dreams. He had the help of two magical birds. Every morning his birds traveled to all the realms. They returned each night, reporting everything they saw and heard.

As the god of war and lord of Valhalla, Odin oversaw the souls of dead warriors. Odin had a magical spear named Gungnir. This spear never missed and always killed its targets. In this way, Odin never lost a battle—until he met his destiny in Ragnarok.

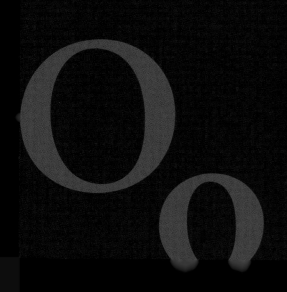

O is for Odin

Wise one-eyed Odin
was the all-father;
he was god of war
and lord of Valhalla.

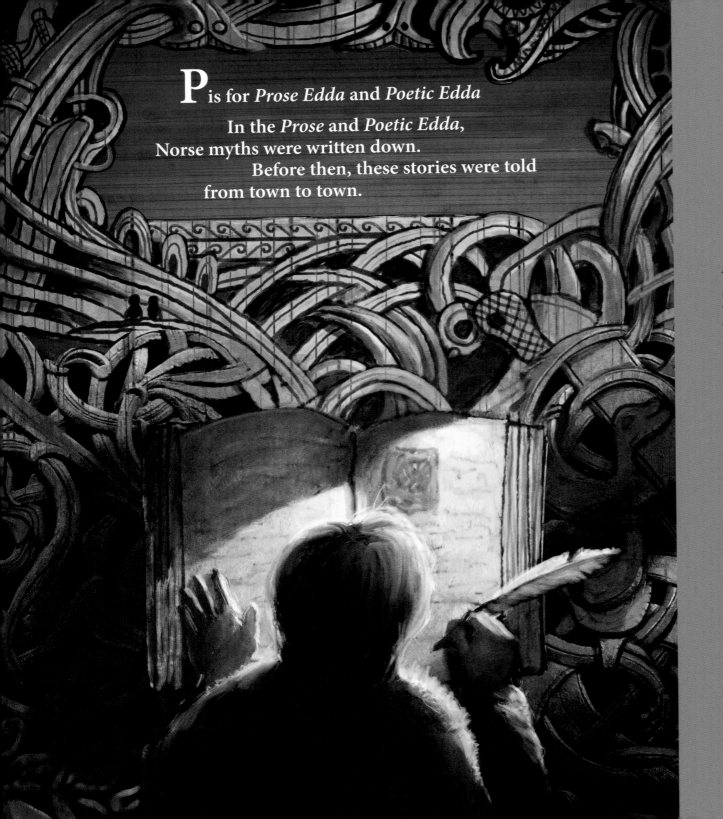

P is for *Prose Edda* and *Poetic Edda*

In the *Prose* and *Poetic Edda*,
Norse myths were written down.
Before then, these stories were told
from town to town.

The *Prose* and *Poetic Edda* are the main sources of the Norse myths. *Edda* means "great-grandmother." One theory is that these texts are like a great-grandmother's stories, containing passed-down knowledge and tales. Another theory is that *Edda* sounds like "Oddi," which is the name of Snorri Sturluson's hometown.

Sturluson, an Icelandic historian, poet, and politician, wrote or compiled the *Prose Edda* in the early thirteenth century as a handbook to Icelandic poetry. It's called *Prose* because Sturluson included explanations of the poetry. But the *Prose Edda* is most famous for its tales about the Norse gods and goddesses. It's called the *Younger Edda* because it draws from stories heard from townspeople and the *Poetic Edda* as its primary sources. Sturluson added many of his own embellishments.

The *Poetic Edda* is the name for a collection of old Norse poems about Norse myths and legends, passed down orally through generations. The author of the *Poetic Edda* is unknown but it is believed to have been written before the *Prose Edda* and is called the *Elder Edda*. Together, the texts provide much of what we know about Scandinavian mythology, history, and religion.

As Odin's wife, Frigg was the queen of Asgard. She was the goddess of marriage, childbirth, motherhood, and fertility. She loved her children more than anything in the world. She had twin sons named Balder and Hod and many stepchildren from Odin's relationships with other goddesses, giantesses, and humans.

Frigg often sat next to Odin's throne in Valaskjalf, one of Odin's halls in Asgard. Frigg's and Odin's thrones were the highest seats, overlooking all the realms. Frigg was second in command and was often in charge when Odin went on his many adventures. She had her own hall called Fensalir, which means "marsh hall." She lived with at least twelve maidens, who assisted her with her work. For example, after Frigg decided who or what deserved her protection, Hlin, the goddess of refuge, provided this protection.

Frigg had many powers. One of them was magical weaving. She couldn't control fate, but she did have a special spinning wheel made of stars. She pulled yarn from the clouds to make golden threads for the gods' clothes. She could also weave clouds, sunshine, and rain in order to grow crops.

Q is for Queen of Asgard
As a wife and mother, Frigg was
generous and kind.
As a goddess and queen,
she knew her own mind.

R r

The peace between the gods and giants broke after Balder's death. Without his light, Fimbulwinter, a fierce winter, began and lasted three years. Fimbulwinter started Ragnarok, which was known as the final battle, the end of the world, and the "twilight of the gods."

After Fimbulwinter, earthquakes came, breaking the shackles that held Loki and monsters in the underworld. All the evil in the world was unleashed. Fire giants attacked Bifrost, causing Heimdall to sound the Gjallerhorn. Roosters crowed warnings to the realms. The gods heard Heimdall's call and prepared for battle. They met at the Well of Urd to receive final blessings from the Norns. Odin also went to Mimisbrunnr to seek counsel from Mimir.

Odin and Freya summoned their armies of dead warrior souls. All the beings of the nine realms readied their weapons. Now an enemy of the gods, Loki led an army of frost giants and fought against the Aesir. They fought at a battlefield called Vigrid, which means "place on which battle surges." At Vigrid, Loki and Heimdall killed each other. Most myths say they were the last gods to die in Ragnarok. And, as destined, all the Norse realms were destroyed in the battle.

R is for Ragnarok

Gods, giants, and monsters
who were doomed to die,
fought as foretold
even as flames filled the sky.

S is for Surtr

Setting the realms ablaze
with his sword of fire,
Surtr turned the Norse world
into a funeral pyre.

Surtr, a fire giant whose name means "black soot," was the guardian of Muspell, the realm of fire. He was stationed at its gates. After Fimbulwinter and the earthquakes, the sky opened and there was a crack. Surtr and other fire giants burst through this crack and attacked Asgard. They rode on horseback across Bifrost and broke the bridge. It was Surtr's attack that caused Heimdall to blow the Gjallerhorn.

After destroying Bifrost, Surtr led the charge to the battlefield. He had a magical sword of blindingly brilliant fire that burned all in its path. With this flaming sword, Surtr battled Frey. Since Frey had traded his magical sword in order to marry Gerd, he was no match for Surtr. Frey was the first of the Aesir gods to die in Ragnarok.

Surtr killed Frey and then rampaged throughout the realms, setting everything on fire. He wiped out most of the gods, giants, and humans, turning them to ashes. He eventually died from the wounds he suffered in his battle with Frey.

S s

T is for Thor

Of all the Norse gods,
        Thor is the most known;
nothing can stop him
        once his hammer is thrown.

Tt

Thor was the god of thunder, lightning, and storms. His father was Odin and his mother was Jord, a giantess. He lived in a large hall named Bilskirnir, which means "lightning crack." He never went anywhere without his famous unbreakable hammer. Made by dwarfs, it was named Mjollnir, which means "the crusher." The hammer could level mountains, always destroying its target. It never missed and could find its way back to Thor. It could also grow or shrink as needed. Thor needed special iron gloves to lift Mjollnir. He also had a magical belt, which doubled his power.

Thor was often sent to fight giants. A formidable opponent, he killed more than any other god. In one myth, a giant stole Mjollnir and demanded Freya's hand in marriage in exchange for the hammer's return. With Loki's help, Thor dressed as Freya and pretended to marry the giant, only to kill him with Mjollnir on the wedding night.

Thor was killed by Jormungundr, a giant world serpent, during Ragnarok. Thor crushed Jormungundr with his hammer, but the venomous monster had already bitten him before dying. Thor walked back nine steps before falling to the ground, choking on Jormungundr's venom.

Helheim was the home of the dead and located in Niflheim. It was also home to monstrous creatures imprisoned there. Hel, ruler of Helheim, had a body that was half living, half dead. She and her two brothers—Fenrir and Jormungundr—were the monster children of Loki and a giantess. Hel and Fenrir were banished to Helheim at birth. Jormungundr was banished to the sea. The Aesir feared them because Odin predicted they would destroy the gods.

Jormungundr's serpent body was wrapped around Midgard. After Fimbulwinter, Jormungundr headed to the surface, causing earthquakes and floods. Fenrir was a giant wolf that kept growing. In Helheim, he was shackled by magical chains. In some myths, when released during Ragnarok, Fenrir ran around the world eating everything in his way, including the sun. He killed Odin, swallowing him and his army. One of Odin's sons killed Fenrir, avenging Odin's death. During Ragnarok, Hel gave Loki an army of dead soldiers. She also gave him a ship made from the fingernails and toenails of Helheim's dead. Manned by the souls of dead giants, Hel's ship could sail over the flooded world.

U is for Underworld Creatures

Monsters were banished
        to the underworld.
When Ragnarok came,
        their rage was unfurled.

Uu

Valkyries, whose name means "choosers of the slain," were mystical female beings. They were thought to have once been human daughters of royals or great warriors. Odin chose them, trained them to be warriors, and gave them magical powers. According to some myths, they rode on winged horses. In other myths, they rode on winged swans or sprouted wings of their own.

Their main responsibility was to fly around battlefields in groups of nine and, on Odin's behalf, choose which warriors would die and which would live, based on how bravely they fought. Then, among the dead, they decided who went to Odin in Valhalla and who went to Freya in Sessrumnir. These dead warriors' souls trained all day to prepare for Ragnarok. At night, the Valkyries served them magical drinks that made them stronger, healed their wounds, and improved their memories.

In some myths, they served as magical weavers. Unlike the Norns, who weaved the fates of living beings, Valkyries weaved the fates of dead warriors, using the warriors' intestines as thread, and severed heads, swords, and arrows as looms. By weaving, they chose where the dead souls would go. Valkyries also served as Odin's bodyguards and messengers.

Vv

V is for Valkyries

These young maidens
were dark angels of death,
deciding which warriors
would take their last breath.

Ægir, a sea giant, and his wife, Ran, were allies of the gods and ruled over the icy, stormy northern seas. They lived in a grand hall at the bottom of the sea. They had nine daughters, who were known as the Nine Waves. The Nine Waves had the powers of the ocean and were named for specific types of waves. For example, one daughter's name meant a hidden wave, while another's meant a foamy wave.

The sisters loved each other and shared an unbreakable alliance. In some myths, all Nine Waves fell in love with Odin and gave birth to Heimdall. In other versions, only one of them had a son with Odin, while the other eight waves helped to cover it up to avoid punishment from their parents.

All Nine Waves raised Heimdall. They fed him soil, seawater, and the sun's heat. Heimdall grew tall and strong. Then he left his mothers to go serve Odin in Asgard. As one of the last gods to die in Ragnarok, Heimdall's power to see the future gave him the knowledge that the world would be reborn.

W
W

W is for Waves

Nine sisters lived in the sea,
each a powerful wave;
they gave birth to Heimdall
in an underwater cave.

X

x

Norse mythology is part of Scandinavian folklore. Scandinavia is a region in northern Europe. It covers the kingdoms of Denmark, Norway, Sweden, Finland, and the island of Iceland. These countries are also often referred to as Nordic countries.

Vikings were Norse seamen and shipbuilders. They were fierce warriors who explored the seas and raided across Europe in the eighth to eleventh centuries. They were known as pirates, traders, and settlers. They began combats by throwing spears at opposing armies and thus, dedicated the battle to Odin. They believed those who survived only did so by Odin's grace and for those who died in battle, it meant Odin would honor their deaths by claiming their souls.

Vikings were devoted to the Norse gods and goddesses and told their stories, passing them down orally from person to person. They gathered in large halls to listen to stories, songs, and poetry. The Norse worldview consists of four phases: the process in which the world was created, the time when gods lived, the destruction of the world in Ragnarok, and the rising of a new world from the sea.

X is for X Marks the Spot—Scandinavia

Vikings came from
Scandinavian lands.
They raided and traded
and made demands.

Yy

Yggdrasil, the world tree, was an eternally green enormous ash tree. It held the realms of the Norse world together. Asgard and Vanaheim, where the gods lived, were in its upper branches. The realm of Gimle, which means "high heavens," was also in the upper branches. Around the center of the trunk, the giants and trolls lived in Jotunheim and the elves lived in Alfheim. Mortals lived in Midgard, which was by the trunk near the ground, surrounded by a sea. Among Yggdrasil's roots lived the dwarfs in Svartalfheim, the fire giants in Muspell, and the dead in Niflheim.

Yggdrasil had three roots. The first went to Asgard, next to the Norns' Well of Urd. The second went to Jotunheim, next to Mimisbrunnr. The third went to Niflheim, next to the well, Hvergelmir, which means "bubbling cauldron." Several creatures lived on Yggdrasil, including a dragon, an eagle, and a squirrel. The eagle and dragon hated each other and the squirrel zigzagged up and down the tree, conveying their insults. At the start of Ragnarok, Yggdrasil trembled as Jormungundr emerged from the sea. The trembling caused the earthquakes that led to the destruction of the world.

Y is for Yggdrasil

Yggdrasil was a special tree,
  known for more than just its fruits.
All the worlds and realms were held
  within its branches and its roots.

Z is for Zest

Two humans named
Life and Life's Zest
    hid in the world tree,
        safe from the rest.

Jormungundr's rising from the sea submerged all nine realms. Meanwhile, Surtr's fires raged on, turning almost everything to ashes. When the fires and floodwaters met, steam rose and filled the air. Ragnarok was over and the Norse world ended as it had started, with fire and ice.

The sun, which had been eaten by Fenrir, was replaced by another, and a new fertile world surfaced from the waters. Yggdrasil, burnt and bruised, was still alive as it was immune to Surtr's fires. Inside its trunk hid two human survivors: a woman named Lif meaning "life," and a man named Lifthrasir meaning "life's zest." They repopulated the earth and are believed to be the ancestors of today's people.

A handful of gods did survive; they included two of Odin's sons and two of Thor's sons. In addition, Balder and Hod, who had broken free from the underworld during the earthquakes to help fight in Ragnarok, survived. They served as reminders to the new world that gods once ruled over all. Though Ragnarok was the destruction of the Norse mythological world, the stories of Odin, Thor, Loki, and the others are still being told and enjoyed to this day.

Z z

Norse Connections

Did you know ....?

There are many movies, television shows, and video games based on Norse mythology. Some aspects of our modern world have even been influenced by it.

Some believe the days of the week are named after Norse gods and goddesses.

* Sunday is named for Sol, goddess of the sun.

* Monday is named for Mani, goddess of the moon.

* Tuesday is named for Tyr, god of war.

* Wednesday is Woden's Day, which is named for Odin. (In some myths, Odin is referred to as Woden.)

* Thursday is named for Thor, god of thunder.

* Friday is named for Frigg or Freya.

* Saturday does not have a Norse connection; it's named for Saturn, an ancient Roman god of peace and plenty.

Some believe that Christmas traditions are connected to Norse myths.

* Thor is connected to Christmas trees. Thor's Oak was a sacred tree located in Hesse, Germany. In the eighth century, a British missionary named Saint Boniface saw a group of pagans making sacrifices to Thor before this oak tree. He wanted to convert the pagans to Christianity by showing them that his god was greater than Thor. So Boniface cut down this tree and used the wood from the tree to build a church. A new tree grew from the stump. Christians interpreted this as rebirth and from then on, evergreen trees were used to celebrate the birth of Jesus Christ. (Christmas trees may also pay homage to Yggdrasil.)

* In order to see the world as humans see it, Odin traveled to Midgard and disguised himself as a tall man wearing a cloak and hat with a long white beard. In some stories, he was called "Long Beard." Odin may have inspired our conception of Saint Nicolas (or Nicholas), otherwise known as Santa Claus.

But wait, there's more!

✳ There are space objects named after characters in Norse myths. For example, the Norse group, a large group of Saturn's moons, orbit in the opposite direction of Saturn's rotation. They may also have irregular orbits that are more elongated than circular. Many of these moons are named after Norse giants. One of the moons is named Fenrir, after the giant wolf. This moon was believed to be captured by Saturn's gravity.

✳ The Minnesota Vikings is a professional American football team. They use a large horn called the "Gjallerhorn" during home games to signal the arrival of the football players and the start of the battle between two football teams. In 2019, the owners of the Minnesota Vikings created a new professional eSports team to compete in video-game competitions. The name of this team is the Minnesota Røkkr (/rock-er/), which means "twilight," a reference to Ragnarok.

✳ A Note from the Author ✳

Ancient Norse people told stories to entertain each other and to explain things that they did not have the science to understand at the time. For example, they were awed by thunder and lightning. During storms, Norse people looked to the skies and believed Thor was slaying giants with his hammer as he rode across the sky in his chariot. The scientific explanation is that thunder is a sound that is caused by lightning, which is a bolt of electricity that shoots through the air, making air vibrate. These vibrations are heard as sounds or thunder. Luckily, today we have both Norse myths and science to help us learn about the world!

Norse myths illustrate the Viking warrior spirit. These stories inspired the ancient Norse people to be strong and brave, even when faced with uncertainty. Ancient Norse people lived in tough times. They faced long, cold winter nights and endless summer days. They had to fight hard to survive as Scandinavian countries mainly consisted of mountains, volcanoes, snow, and ice. They had scarce resources and had to raid and pillage for food and goods. Norse myths tend to be dark stories, stories of gods who are doomed to die but yet fight until the end. Ancient Norse people both feared and respected their gods; their reverence is evident in the Norse myths, which I'm thrilled to be sharing with you.

Writing about myths is challenging. Like folktales and urban legends, myths are passed down via oral traditions. This means that each storyteller may embellish by adding or changing details. Historians and writers (like me) use various sources and make decisions based on consistencies among various retellings. Regardless, Norse myths, in all their versions, will always intrigue and fascinate.

This book is dedicated to my Book Club Goddesses, some of whom may have Norse blood:
Cindy Clevenger, Deborah Halverson, Lynn Kelley, Kathy Krull, Janet Lutz, Barbara Melkerson, Barbara Patton, and Vicky Reed.

—Virginia

To kids and parents all around the world who read lots of books: You're important. And awesome.

—Torstein

Text Copyright © 2020 Virginia Loh-Hagan
Illustration Copyright © 2020 Torstein Nordstrand
Design Copyright © 2020 Sleeping Bear Press

All rights reserved. No part of this book may be reproduced in any manner
without the express written consent of the publisher, except in the case of brief
excerpts in critical reviews and articles. All inquiries should be addressed to:

SLEEPING BEAR PRESS™

2395 South Huron Parkway, Suite 200
Ann Arbor, MI 48104
www.sleepingbearpress.com

Printed and bound in the United States.

Library of Congress Cataloging-in-Publication Data

Names: Loh-Hagan, Virginia, author. | Nordstrand, Torstein, illustrator.
Title: T is for Thor : a Norse mythology alphabet / written by Virginia Loh Hagan
and illustrated by Torstein Nordstrand.
Description: Ann Arbor, MI : Sleeping Bear Press, 2020. | Audience: Ages 6-10 |
Summary: "An alphabetical exploration of Scandinavian mythology, history, culture,
and religion, examining famous gods such as Loki, Thor, and Odin, as well as
lesser-known inhabitants of this nine-realm universe"—Provided by publisher.
Identifiers: LCCN 2020006356 | ISBN 9781534110502 (hardcover)
Subjects: LCSH: Mythology, Norse—Juvenile literature. | Alphabet books.
Classification: LCC BL860 .L64 2020 | DDC 293/.13--dc23
LC record available at https://lccn.loc.gov/2020006356